Swords to Plowshares

The Creation of John P. Klassen's
Mennonite Central Committee Medallion

"Swords Into Plowshares," bronze plaque, 1930s, 38" x 16", John P. Klassen
Klassen Court, Bluffton University

Swords to Plowshares

The Creation of John P. Klassen's
Mennonite Central Committee Medallion

Story by Lisa Weaver
Illustrations by Amanda Huston

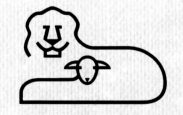

The Lion and Lamb Peace Arts Center
of Bluffton University

To Mom and Dad – LW
To my family – AH

The Lion and Lamb Peace Arts Center
Bluffton University
1 University Drive, Bluffton, Ohio 45817
www.bluffton.edu/lionlamb

Weaver, Lisa D.
    Swords to Plowshares / story by Lisa Weaver; illustrations by Amanda Huston; design by Alison King.

ISBN 978-0-615-95157-7

Library of Congress Control Number: 2014932001

Introduction

Beginning in 1789, Mennonites lived and prospered in the southern part of the Russian empire, now Ukraine. Mennonites had come from Prussia (now a part of Poland) at the invitation of Catherine the Great, the ruler of Russia. In exchange for developing and populating her southern lands, Catherine offered the Mennonites freedom of religion, including the important belief of conscientious objection to military service. Mennonites established farms and villages, raised wheat and other crops, planted orchards of fruit trees, started agricultural industries, created schools and hospitals and worshiped without fear of persecution.

This peaceful way of life was shattered by the Russian Revolution of 1917 and the civil war that ensued. Opposing armies fought back and forth over the area where the Mennonite villages stood. In addition, roving bands of anarchists plundered the countryside. Many people in these villages were killed. Crops were destroyed and farm animals were slaughtered. Horses were confiscated by armies, and without them to pull the plows, no new crops could be planted. This soon resulted in famine. Later, the spread of diseases such as typhus claimed many more lives throughout Russia.

Mennonites living in the United States and Canada soon learned of the suffering of their brothers and sisters across the ocean and wanted to help. In 1920 they established the Mennonite Central Committee as an organization to send relief supplies including food, clothing, tractors and plows. This relief effort saved many people—both Mennonites and their neighbors—from starvation. Churches in the region sent numerous letters of appreciation for this help. In addition, John P. Klassen, an art teacher living in one of the Mennonite villages that received aid, made a medallion. Based on these facts, this book is a fictionalized account of the making of that medallion.

We will now begin our story in the village of Chortitza …

Twelve-year-old Isaak sat in the branches of the massive oak tree that grew near his home, one skinny leg hanging down, swinging back and forth. He liked being up among the leaves, hidden from view. It was a safe, strong tree, and well-known to all the villagers around – the tree was of immense proportions and said to be 700 years old.

Isaak peered out through the branches of the great oak. It was almost time for him to go to school. He went early every morning to help Mr. Klassen in his art room. Mr. Klassen taught in the Teachers College, just a couple doors up from Isaak's own school. Isaak's art teacher, Mr. Dyck, had told Mr. Klassen that Isaak would be a good helper for him.

7

Each morning, Isaak swept the art room floor carefully and washed the chalkboard. He would then help Mr. Klassen collect all the paintbrushes and straighten up the other art tools. It pleased Isaak to see the room all ready for the day. But what Isaak liked most was when, after the chores were done, Mr. Klassen would beckon him to the art table. Mr. Klassen would pick up a piece of modeling clay, and in just moments, he could create a miniature animal that looked so real that Isaak thought it might jump up and run away. Mr. Klassen especially liked to make horses – big farm horses or nice riding horses. Isaak worked with the clay, too, trying to get his fingers to do what Mr. Klassen's hands did so easily. Sometimes Mr. Klassen and Isaak would sketch little figures of people or animals on scraps of paper.

Below are some of John Klassen's early sketches of horses.

But Isaak wasn't in the art room yet this morning. First he had to take the rather long walk from the oak tree to the school. He took a deep breath and summoned his courage to leave the refuge of the tree. For now came the part he didn't like so much – walking through the streets where the bandits and soldiers had been just a few months previously. They were gone now, but the burned-out shells of houses reminded him of those terrible days of looting and killing. Isaak lowered himself from branch to branch until he was able to drop to the ground.

At his feet lay an acorn. Isaak picked it up and put it into his pocket, as he often did when he found an interesting object. Then, straightening his shoulders, Isaak set off for the school that was on the boundary between the twin villages of Chortitza and Rosental. When he got close, Isaak saw that Mr. Klassen was also approaching and had almost reached the door. Isaak broke into a run, and they arrived at the same moment.

Below are leaves from the great oak tree in Chortitza. John Klassen's son, Paul, brought these home after a trip to Chortitza.

In recent decades, people have traveled to Ukraine to see the Chortitza oak. Many have gathered acorns to plant in the places they now call home.

13

"*Guten Morgen*, Mr. Klassen," panted Isaak.

"*Guten Morgen*, Isaak," replied Mr. Klassen. Then he added, "I see the spring is back in your legs. You are running again."

"Yes, Mr. Klassen," answered Isaak.

John Klassen drew sketches of children receiving food from Mennonite Central Committee workers.

And Isaak knew it was true. Ever since the bread kitchen had opened in the village, he had enough to eat again. Isaak loved the hot chocolate, the taste of the cooked beans and the aroma of the bread baking in the ovens. Mother and father said the food sent by the Mennonite Central Committee in North America had saved them and many other people from starvation. Though the memory of those hungry days would never leave him, the tired feeling in his legs and the dull ache in his belly were now gone.

As Mr. Klassen reached for the keys to unlock the door, a metallic glint on the ground caught Isaak's eye.

Isaak bent down and saw that it was a bullet, left from all the shooting that had taken place in the village. He reached to pick it up. Before he could put it into his pocket, however, Mr. Klassen asked to see it. Isaak gave it to the teacher, wondering if he had done something wrong. Maybe he shouldn't have touched the bullet. Isaak knew that those bullets had been used by the soldiers and bandits to hurt and kill people in the village. Maybe he should have left the bullet alone. But Mr. Klassen did not reprimand him. Instead, Mr. Klassen was studying the bullet carefully and looked as though he was thinking about something. Then he handed the bullet back to Isaak and started peering all around the edge of the building and behind the bushes. "What is he doing?" thought Isaak.

Soon Mr. Klassen had found and picked up a few other bullets like the one Isaak had discovered, and he said, "Come on in – we have work to do."

But when they entered the art room, there was no mention of the broom or dustpan. Instead, Mr. Klassen went immediately to his art table and began drawing a picture. Soon he had sketched a man with a basket of bread on one arm, offering a loaf of bread to three children. Then Mr. Klassen made another drawing, this time of a steamship pushing through the ocean waves. Seeing that, Isaak could imagine himself on the ship's deck watching the water and feeling the wind on his face.

Though he didn't know what it had to do with the bullets Mr. Klassen had carried in, he suddenly thought he knew what Mr. Klassen was drawing. "Why, that's Mr. Slagel, the Mennonite Central Committee worker who brought food to our village," Isaak said in surprise, pointing at the man carrying bread. "And I guess that must be the ship that brought supplies from North America," he continued, now gesturing toward the ship.

Mr. Klassen smiled wisely and nodded, keeping his eyes on the paper as he worked. He added some details: buttons on the man's coat, a flag on the ship and smoke coming from the smokestacks. By then it was time for Isaak to go to his own school. He left the room with slow steps – he would much rather stay to watch Mr. Klassen draw than go to his own class.

Below is a photo of the tools John Klassen used. Take a close look at the initials IK carved into the tool on the left. John Klassen signed Ivan Klassen in the early days.

The next morning, Isaak did not climb into the tree but waited in the shade by the solid trunk. When it was time to go, he did not hesitate at all. He was too curious to see what Mr. Klassen would do. Would he draw more of Mr. Slagel and the ship?

But no pencils emerged today. This morning, Mr. Klassen took up a lump of modeling clay and began shaping a round, flat disk, about the size of the palm of his hand and about as thick as Isaak's little finger.

Then Mr. Klassen picked up some of his modeling tools. These were made of wood, each with a slightly different shape. Isaak watched, fascinated, as the images of the man and the children were now created on the disk. Mr. Klassen then made a second disk, the same size as the first. Soon the supply ship was sailing across its clay surface, just as it had been drawn on the scrap of paper.

It was only then that Mr. Klassen spoke. "It's time for you to go to school now," he said. "But tomorrow we can continue our work of turning swords into plowshares."

Swords into plowshares?

What was Mr. Klassen talking about?

Isaak's classes seemed to stretch on forever that day. How could he concentrate on reading and math when his mind was spinning with images of swords and plows, ships, bullets and baskets of bread?

What is a plowshare?
A plowshare is the part of a plow that cuts the furrow, the long row where seeds are planted.

Early plows were either pushed by hand or pulled behind a team of horses.

That evening at home, Isaak told his mother and father about finding the bullet and about the artwork that Mr. Klassen was creating. When Isaak got to the part about swords and plowshares, he said, perplexed, "What do you think Mr. Klassen was talking about?"

Isaak's mother looked thoughtful for a moment, and then replied, "Bring our Bible, Isaak."

When Isaak handed the Bible to his mother, she turned to the book of Isaiah. She located chapter 2, verse 4, and read aloud:

> *"They shall beat their swords into plowshares, and their spears into pruning hooks; nation shall not lift up sword against nation, neither shall they learn war anymore."*

Isaak's mother looked up from her reading. "Swords to plowshares," she said. "I think Mr. Klassen is saying he wants to change violence into goodness. But I don't know how he will do that. We'll just have to wait and see."

The following morning dawned bright and clear. Isaak awoke and jumped out of bed. He could hardly wait to see what Mr. Klassen would do today. This morning, Isaak did not even stop at the big oak. He ran straight to the school where he waited by the door, hopping back and forth impatiently from one foot to the other.

When Mr. Klassen appeared, Isaak could not contain his curiosity any longer. Instead of the polite "*Guten Morgen*" he had been taught to say, he blurted out, "How are we turning swords into plowshares like Isaiah said in the Bible?"

Mr. Klassen chuckled. "I see you have been doing a lot of thinking."

Inside the art room, Mr. Klassen picked up the clay disks he had made the day before. "I think we should make a medallion like this to give to Mennonite Central Committee," he said. "It can be a small 'thank you' for all the good food and the plows and tractors they sent to us. The other day, I was thinking about how to make a medallion, but I couldn't figure out where I was going to find any good metal. When I saw you pick up that bullet by the door, I realized that we had a supply of lead right at our feet. We will be melting bullets to make a medallion – a medallion that is a symbol of Christian love."

31

And that was the start of a very exciting week for Isaak. He was early to the art room every morning. He couldn't wait to see what the next amazing step would be in the making of the medallion.

One morning he helped Mr. Klassen make the first mold that would be needed. They measured out a pan of water and added some plaster of paris until it formed a thick liquid. Then, with some more clay, they made a little form around the first disk and filled it with the plaster.

Below is one of the molds that John Klassen used in his work, along with the finished piece that was made from the mold.

When the design includes a word or phrase, all of the words will read backward in the mold. On the finished piece, they will all read correctly. Look closely. Can you tell which one is the mold?

CHORTITZA-ROSENTAL
1922

They did the same for the second disk. The following day, they could lift the clay out and see the molds they had created. The most difficult part came when Mr. Klassen carefully carved out the lettering around each image. Isaak could only watch and wonder how anyone could make such perfect lettering. And Mr. Klassen had to make each letter backward in the mold so the words would read correctly after being cast.

After using the molds to make two plaster medallions, Mr. Klassen told Isaak they would now have to make another mold to cast the lead medallion. To do this, he put the two plaster medallions together so they fit back to back. When they were just right – like a big coin with a front and a back side – they cast another mold around them. Mr. Klassen said this one had to be made thicker and stronger to contain the hot lead they would pour into it. And it would have to dry very thoroughly to make sure that all the water was baked out of it; otherwise, it would crack.

Finally the day came that they had been waiting for – the day to melt the bullets and cast the lead medallion. Mr. Klassen got out the bullets he had picked up from around the school, and also showed Isaak some others that had been dug out of the walls of nearby homes. A few more had come from a nearby field where armies had battled. Isaak decided to add his bullet to the collection, too.

Melting the bullets would take a hot, hot stove. Isaak wondered if the bullets would really melt. At first they just lay there in the bottom of the little iron pot. But finally they began to sputter and lose their clear edges. A little melted lead started to pool around them. Sure enough, after a long time there were no bullets left – just a silvery gray liquid. Mr. Klassen carefully poured the melted lead into the hole that they had made at the top of the mold. When it was completely full, Mr. Klassen said they would have to wait until the next day before they could see if their casting was a success.

That evening, Isaak described to his mother and father how they had melted the bullets and poured them into the mold. When the story was finished, Isaak's father said, "A lot of people wondered why John Klassen left the big farm where he grew up and studied to become an artist. I was one of those who questioned his decision. Now I am beginning to understand why it is important for the world to have artists. John Klassen could see a way to transform fear into courage, and despair into hope."

"Swords to plowshares," said Isaak's mother softly.
"Bullets melted down to say 'thank you' for bread."
A tear slid down her cheek as she hugged Isaak to
her side and kissed his forehead.

Early sketches of the medallion.

German words on the medallion translated to English:

Thank the brethren beyond the ocean. We were hungry and you have fed us.

The following morning, Mr. Klassen let Isaak help open the mold. They slipped a knife between the two edges and pried it apart. Inside lay the gleaming medallion. Isaak could see the man passing out food to the children, and the ship carrying supplies across the ocean. The little girl receiving bread reminded Isaak of his little sister. "Chortitza-Rosental 1922" was spelled out underneath the image.

Mr. Klassen handed the medallion to Isaak to hold. It felt smooth and solid and heavy in his hands. The bullets were no more. Instead was an image of the warm bread that had filled his stomach when he had been so hungry.

Actual medallion front

Actual medallion back

"We have turned swords into plowshares and bullets into bread," said Isaak, looking in wonder, first at the medallion and then at the art teacher.

Mr. Klassen smiled and agreed.

Time and touch have worn away the image on the back of the medallion. If you look carefully, can you still see the ship sailing across the water?

45

Connecting the Dots

Reflection on John P. Klassen by Paul Klassen

The story of making the lead medallion from bullets was just one of many we Klassen children heard from our parents. To us, it was one of many stories describing the momentous events our family had experienced in the Mennonite villages of South Russia. When I mentioned the story to Lisa Weaver, her fertile writer's mind immediately saw the potential for a peace book for children containing an important message. I know that my father, John P. Klassen, would have been very pleased with that, for so much of his art included a moral dimension, and much of it was related to his experiences in Russia.

I was born in the year following my parents' emigration from Russia, and just at the time my father began a long tenure as art professor at Bluffton College, now Bluffton University. I recall, in those early years, a number of Russian Mennonite scholars who came to Bluffton to teach. Also, quite a few came as students. There was a steady flow of these recently displaced people visiting our home. The long conversations we heard in German recounted events and people we would never be able to know. And in a sense it seemed like an imaginary world, although we knew that the events and the people they talked about were very real.

In those early years, just like the child Isaak in the story, I watched spellbound on so many occasions as my father worked with clay and plaster or some other medium to create his works. It was fascinating to see the images being created by his sure hands. So I know that the interaction between the artist and the child that is created in this story is true to life and very authentic.

In 1922 a delegation of the important leaders of the Chortitza-Rosental community presented the lead medallion to P.C. Hiebert, the director of the Mennonite Central Committee, just before he returned to America. The medallion was in gratitude for the food and relief supplies sent by Mennonite Central Committee. The delegation presenting the medallion apologized for the fact that there was no fine metal available to make this medallion of thanks. However, after the recipients realized that it had been made from the very bullets that had caused so much devastation and sorrow, they began to prize it even more than if it had been made of gold or silver. This medallion is now in the collection of the Kauffman Museum in North Newton, Kansas, and can be seen there.

It has been a pleasure for me to assist Lisa as she undertook this project, helping, thereby, to pass on to future generations of children a historical story with an important and beautiful message for today.

Paul Klassen

Donors

Thank you to the many individuals and organizations who contributed financial resources sufficient to fully fund the design and publication costs of this project. This generous support allows all proceeds from the sale of *Swords to Plowshares* to support the mission and programs of The Lion and Lamb Peace Arts Center.

A very special thank you is extended to Dr. Elizabeth Hostetler, founding director of The Lion and Lamb, for her leadership gift and to the following individuals and organizations for their very generous support.

Individuals

Edna and George Dyck
Ronald L. and Phyllis R. Friesen
John and Janet Gundy
James M. and Karen Klassen Harder
Herbert J. and Magrita F. Klassen family
Paul and LaVonne Klassen
Louise and Lawrence Matthews
Jon and Sally Weaver Sommer
Willis and Betty Sommer
Margaret and Richard Weaver
Laura and David Yost

Organizations

Bluffton University, Bluffton, Ohio
Central District Conference of Mennonite Church USA
First Mennonite Church, Bluffton, Ohio
Madison Mennonite Church, Madison, Wisconsin

Author

Lisa Weaver grew up in Bluffton, Ohio. As a girl, she played tag amongst the John P. Klassen sculptures found on the Bluffton campus. Now an elementary school teacher in Madison, Wisconsin, Lisa is drawn to stories of peace witness. Lisa is the author of *Praying With Our Feet* (Herald Press) and *On the Zwieback Trail* (CMU Press).

Illustrator

Amanda Huston grew up near Kidron, Ohio. She studied art and graphic design at Bluffton University, where she received the Distinguished Scholar in Studio Art Award upon graduation. As an artist, she is deeply appreciative of Klassen's art legacy and enjoyed his artwork around campus. In addition to illustrating, Amanda works as a librarian and spends much of her time in the children's department.

Connecting the Dots

Credits and Acknowledgements

Print Resources

Hiebert, P.C. *Feeding the Hungry.* Mennonite Central Committee, 1929.

Klassen, John. "Saved from Starvation by MCC Relief." *The Mennonite.* Volume LX, Number 27. July 10, 1945.

Klassen, John. "Sketches from a Chortitza Boyhood." *Mennonite Life,* December 1973.

Klassen, Paul. "John P. Klassen and the Beginnings of the Art Legacy at Bluffton University." *Mennonite Life,* Spring 2008.

Weaver, Lisa. *On the Zwieback Trail: A Russian Mennonite Alphabet of Stories, Recipes and Historic Events.* CMU Press, 2011.

Note: All sketches reproduced in this book can be found in the December 1973 issue of *Mennonite Life.*

Photos

Photos throughout the book are from the collections of the Kauffman Museum at Bethel College, Alison King, John Klassen, Paul Klassen, and Shutterstock.com. All rights reserved.

A very special thank you from the author to Louise Matthews, director of The Lion and Lamb Peace Arts Center. Without Louise, this book would have remained an idea without a home.

Additional thanks to:

Ron Adams, Andreas Baumgartner, Robin Bowlus, Jonathan Dyck, Hans Houshower, Mary Jean Johnson, Gregg Luginbuhl, Gerald Mast, Rachel Pannabecker, Titus Peachey, Steve Yoder

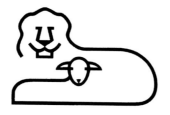

The Lion and Lamb Peace Arts Center
of Bluffton University

Mission of The Lion and Lamb Peace Arts Center

Through all appropriate means, but especially through literature and the arts, The Lion and Lamb Peace Arts Center of Bluffton University promotes the study of peace and justice, cultural understanding and nonviolent responses to conflict with an emphasis on these themes for children.

For more information, visit **www.bluffton.edu/lionlamb/**

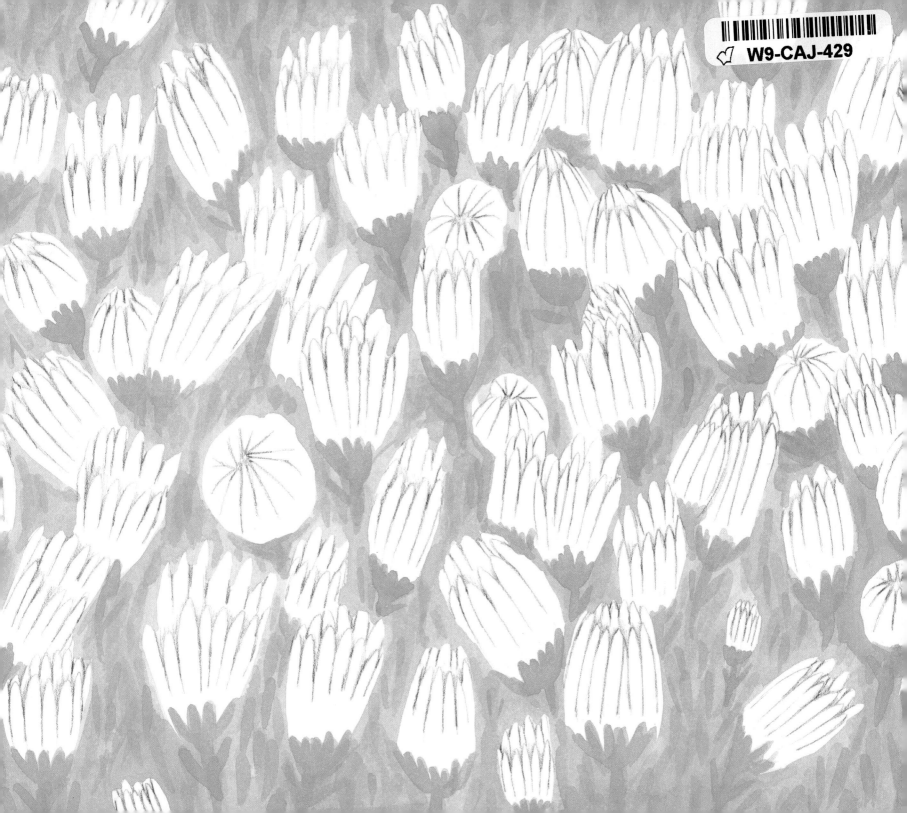

JESSIXA BAGLEY

Daisy

NEAL PORTER BOOKS

HOLIDAY HOUSE / NEW YORK

Neal Porter Books

Text and illustrations copyright © 2021 by Jessixa Bagley
All Rights Reserved
HOLIDAY HOUSE is registered in the U.S. Patent and Trademark Office.
Printed and bound in November 2020 at Leo Paper, Heshan, China.
The artwork for this book was created with watercolor and pencil.
Book design by Jennifer Browne
www.holidayhouse.com
First Edition
10   9   8   7   6   5   4   3   2   1

Library of Congress Cataloging-in-Publication Data

Names: Bagley, Jessixa, author, illustrator.
Title: Daisy / by Jessixa Bagley.
Description: First edition. | New York City : Holiday House, [2021] |
Audience: Ages 4 to 8. | Audience: Grades K-1. | Summary: Because she is
teased at school, Daisy hangs her head a lot, which leads to a new hobby
of collecting lost and broken items and to a real treasure—a new friend.
Identifiers: LCCN 2020017372 | ISBN 9780823446506 (hardcover)
Subjects: CYAC: Teasing—Fiction. | Collectors and collecting—Fiction. |
Friendship—Fiction. | Warthog—Fiction. | Animals—Fiction.
Classification: LCC PZ7.1.B3 Dai 2021 | DDC [E]—dc23
LC record available at https://lccn.loc.gov/2020017372

ISBN 978-0-8234-4650-6 (hardcover)

To the amazing women in my life. You are all my treasures.

Daisy was named after
her mama's favorite flower.

"They seem plain, but when you look closer you see their beauty," her mama would say.

There were times
when she didn't feel
like her name.
Especially at school.

"You don't look like a daisy," said Rose.
"More like a thistle," said Violet smugly.
Hazel and all the rest of the girls laughed.

Daisy put her head down.

She put her head down a lot of the time.

So Daisy made her own fun.

When she looked down, she found
a whole magical world of things
that seemed overlooked,
just like her.

Treasures that were once special and
adored, now forgotten, seemed the
most beautiful of all to Daisy.

Those were her prized possessions.

She kept them secret.

No one knew
about Daisy's fort.

It was a magical place, hidden
from the eyes of others.

Buttons, lost marbles, cracked
teacups, old glasses, empty jars,
tin cans with colorful labels . . .

They were old and useless items to others, but to Daisy they were priceless, and she honored and loved each one for its special beauty.

Things were less magical
outside of her fort.
"There goes Thistle looking
for junk again," said Violet.
The others just laughed.

Daisy pretended to be busy looking for treasures. But her head hung so low, all she could see was her feet.

One day after school she returned to her fort and saw a beautiful crystal candy dish outside the entrance.

"How pretty! Where did this come from?" said Daisy.

She placed it among her treasures and went home.

The next day Daisy was out looking for mushrooms for her mother when she came across an old broken saucer in the underbrush.

"Oh, what a lovely find!" she said with excitement. On her way home she stopped by her fort to put her new prize inside.

Once again when she got
there something was waiting
for her.

Daisy held the broken pocket
watch up to her ear and imagined
the soft silvery sounds of the
hands ticking away.

That night, Daisy couldn't sleep.
"Where are all these things coming from?
And why? Will there be something tomorrow?"

Each day after school, Daisy would head to
her fort, and each day there was a new item
to be cherished. But she still didn't know
where they came from.

Until the day
she stayed late
after school.

When she got to her fort,
she heard a rustling sound.

"Hey!" called Daisy.
"What are you doing?"

"I was just leaving this for you," said
the visitor bashfully. "I've seen you looking
around for stuff outside of school."

"Oh. Most people think
I'm silly for liking old junk," she
said, keeping her head down.

"Junk? I think they're treasures!"
the visitor whispered.

Daisy lifted up her head.

"Hi, I'm Fern."

"I'm Daisy," she said with a smile.

"Would you like to go for a walk?"
said Fern. "Maybe we'll find something
special along the way."

"I bet we will," said Daisy.